# The Wizard Of Oz

A PARRAGON BOOK

Published by
Parragon Books,
Unit 13-17, Avonbridge Trading Estate,
Atlantic Road, Avonmouth, Bristol BS11 9QD

Produced by
The Templar Company plc,
Pippbrook Mill, London Road, Dorking, Surrey RH4 1JE



Designed by Mark Kingsley-Monks

Printed and bound in Italy

ISBN 0-75250-939-X

# The Wizard Of Oz

Retold by Stephanie Laslett
Illustrated by Martin Orme

Dorothy lived with her little dog, Toto, her Uncle and her Aunt on a farm in the middle of a great prairie. Their little house had just one room inside, with a trapdoor leading to a cellar. One day when Dorothy was playing in the yard, the sky turned dark.

"Hurry!" cried Uncle Henry. "Run to the cellar. There's a cyclone coming!" Dorothy ran towards the trapdoor but to her dismay poor terrified Toto jumped from her arms and hid under the bed.

"Come here, Toto!" cried Dorothy but her voice was lost in the wailing shriek of the tornado. Suddenly the whole house shook. The mighty wind had picked it up, whirled it around three times and was carrying it away in the eye of the storm.

Dorothy's eyes grew as round as saucers as her home sped across the sky. After a time it seemed to be falling and then suddenly it landed with a bump upon the ground. The little girl ran outside and the first thing she saw was a pair of silver slippers sticking out from beneath the verandah.

"Oh, thank you for killing the Wicked Witch of the East and setting us free," cried a small voice.

Dorothy turned round and was astonished to see a group of strange little people smiling up at her.

"Welcome to the Land of the Munchkins," said a lady in a pink pointed hat. Dorothy looked very shocked. "Was she a *real* Witch?" she asked fearfully. The lady laughed.

"Why, yes," she replied, "And so am I! But she was a bad witch and I am a good one. My name is the Witch of the North. The Witch of the South is also good, but the Witch of the West is horrid." The Munchkins laughed merrily as Dorothy shook her head in total bewilderment.

“Things are different here in the Land of Oz,” smiled the good Witch. “We even have our very own Wizard.” But Dorothy was busy thinking of her own home back on the farm. “I would like to go home now,” she said politely, but the Munchkins shook their heads sadly.

“There is no way out of Oz,” explained the Witch, “but perhaps the Wizard could help you. You must follow the Yellow Brick Road to the Emerald City. You will need good luck so here is my kiss on your forehead to protect you and here are the silver shoes that the Wicked Witch of the East used to wear.”

The slippers were a perfect fit and soon Dorothy and Toto were on their way along the Yellow Brick Road. After a while they passed a Scarecrow perched high on a pole above a field of corn.

"How do you do?" asked Dorothy.

"I do not know," replied the Scarecrow, "because my head is stuffed with straw. How I wish I had a head full of brains."

"Come with me to see the Wizard of Oz," said Dorothy. "Maybe he can help you." So together they set off down the Yellow Brick Road.

After a while they came across a strange man made all of tin. He looked very sad and they asked him what was wrong. "I have no heart and I would so love one," he said.

"Come with us to see the Wizard of Oz," invited Dorothy and the Tin Woodman very gladly agreed.

Next, they passed through a dark wood and a large Lion suddenly jumped out and roared at Toto. Dorothy ran forward and smacked the Lion hard on the nose.

"What's a big beast like you doing scaring a little dog like Toto! Why, you are nothing but a coward!" she cried.

The Lion hung his head in shame. "You are right," he admitted. "I am scared of almost everything. How I wish I could be brave."

Soon he, too, had joined them on their journey. "Perhaps the Wizard will give me courage," said the Lion.

They travelled many miles until at last they reached the beautiful Emerald City. Here in a great green palace lived the Wizard of Oz.

"I am Oz, the Great and Terrible," he thundered. "What do you want?"

Each explained in turn what they most desired and at last the Wizard spoke. "First you must kill the Witch of the West," he ordered.

The four friends comforted one another. "None of us wants to kill the Witch, however bad she might be," sighed Dorothy, "but I suppose we must try and find her or we will never have our wishes." And so they set off towards the setting sun with fear in their hearts.

Now the Wicked Witch of the West had magic powers. She saw the travellers as soon as they set foot in her land and sent her Winged Monkeys to attack them.

"Destroy the strangers!" she cried, "but bring me the Lion for he could be useful." The Monkeys swooped down upon the little group and carried off the Scarecrow and the Tin Woodman and dropped them into a deep ravine. They returned for Dorothy but, when they saw the magic mark upon her forehead, they spared her. She and the Lion were captured and taken before the Witch of the West.

"Now I have *two* slaves," cackled the Witch gleefully and she set them to work in the kitchen.

The Witch had spotted Dorothy's magic shoes and vowed they would be hers. The next day she made a grab for them and Dorothy was so angry that she threw her bucket of water at the wicked crone. She did not realise that water was the one thing that could destroy the Witch and so she was astonished to see the old hag melting away.

"We are free!" cried Dorothy. They soon rescued the Scarecrow and the Tin Woodman and set off back to the Emerald City.

Slowly they entered the Palace.
"I am Oz, the Great and Terrible," boomed a loud voice, but the Wizard was nowhere to be seen. Toto ran to a corner of the room and snuffled behind a screen. With a crash, it fell to reveal a little man with a bald head and green glasses.

"Oh, dear! Oh, dear!" he quavered. "Now you know the real truth about the Wizard of Oz! The Wizard is really me — just an ordinary man. I got carried here many years ago when my hot air balloon was blown off course and everyone thought I must be a real Wizard!"

The four friends were horrified. How would they ever get their wishes granted now?

"I will try my best to help you," said the old man and he turned to the Scarecrow. "You have been very clever finding your way about the Land of Oz. Every day you learn something new and that is how you gain brains but, if you wish, here is something to put inside your head." And the man mixed some bran and some new pins and packed them inside the Scarecrow's head. He felt as sharp as a new pin and was so pleased!

Next he carefully placed a silk heart stuffed with sawdust inside the Tin Woodman's chest.

"Now you have a kind heart," he said, "and I hope it makes you happy." The Tin Woodman fancied he could already feel it beating!

Now it was the Lion's turn.

"You have shown that you have plenty of courage," said the old man. "Everyone is afraid when they face danger. All you need is confidence in yourself. Drink this and then you will always have courage inside you." The Lion lapped up a bowl of green liquid.

"Now I feel brave," he roared.

"It's my turn now," said Dorothy eagerly. The little man thought long and hard and at last he spoke.

"I arrived in a hot air balloon, and we shall leave in it! But first you need to help me get it ready." Quickly they set to work.

Soon their beautiful green silk balloon was ready to go but as Dorothy prepared to step inside the basket, the rope snapped and the balloon rose high in the sky without her!

Dorothy wept bitter tears but was soon calmed by a gentle voice.

"Never fear, Dorothy. You shall return home after all." It was the good Witch of the South come to help her. "You had the answer all along," she explained. "Just tap the heels of your silver shoes together three times and they will take you wherever you want to go!"

Soon Dorothy was flying through the air with Toto in her arms.

"Goodbye, dear friends," she called. "I am going home at last!"

In no time at all the farm was in sight and how happy they all were to be together once again.

"The Land of Oz was wonderful," said Dorothy, "but there's no place like home!"

## L. Frank Baum

When *The Wizard of Oz* was first
published in 1900, its author, L. Frank Baum,
felt the time was right for a new kind
of fairy story or "wonder tale" in which "the
wonderment and joy (of fairy tales)
are retained and the heart-ache and
nightmares are left out". It originally began as
a bedtime tale for his four young sons and it is
said that their father had much in common
with the wonderful Wizard himself.
The book was first called *The Emerald City*
but this was quickly changed owing to
superstition which claimed bad luck will
follow a book with a jewel in its title.